-Haunted History-

The Tower of London Is Haunted!

Marie Morrison

PowerKiDS press.

New York

Published in 2021 by The Rosen Publishing Group, Inc.
29 East 21st Street, New York, NY 10010

Portions of this work were originally authored by Drew Nelson and published as *Haunted! The Tower of London.* All new material this edition authored by Marie Morrison.

Editor: Jill Keppeler
Book Design: Rachel Rising

Photo Credits: Cover GParker/Shutterstock.com; Cover, pp.1-32 (background) Slava Gerj/Shutterstock.com; p. 4 Engel Ching/Shutterstock.com; pp. 5, 30 Kiev.Victor/Shutterstock.com; p. 7 Iakov Kalinin/Shutterstock.com; p. 9 Paolo Paradiso/Shutterstock.com; p. 11Print Collector/Contributor/Getty Images; p. 13 DEA/G. DAGLI ORTI/Contributor/Getty Images; p. 15 Elena Elisseeva/Shutterstock.com; p. 17 aaabbbccc/Shutterstock.com; p. 19 Richard Melichar/Shutterstock.com; p. 21 Universal History Archive/Contributor/Getty Images; p. 23 Heritage Images/Contributor/Getty Images; p. 25 Georgios Kollidas/Shutterstock.com; p. 27 chrisdorney/Shutterstock.com; p. 28 Lorena Huerta/Shutterstock.com; p. 29 Gaid Kornsilapa/Shutterstock.com.

Cataloging-in-Publication Data

Names: Morrison, Marie.
Title: The Tower of London is haunted! / Marie Morrison.
Description: New York : PowerKids Press, 2021. | Series: Haunted history | Includes glossary and index.
Identifiers: ISBN 9781725320048 (pbk.) | ISBN 9781725320062 (library bound) | ISBN 9781725320055 (6 pack)
Subjects: LCSH: Tower of London (London, England)--Juvenile literature. | Haunted places--Juvenile literature. | Ghosts--England--Juvenile literature. | London (England)--Buildings, structures, etc.--Juvenile literature.
Classification: LCC BF1475.M67 2021 | DDC 133.1--dc23

Manufactured in the United States of America

CPSIA Compliance Information: Batch #CSPK20. For further information contact Rosen Publishing, New York, New York at 1-800-237-9932.

CONTENTS

THESE OLD STONES

The Tower of London has seen a lot of history. This structure on the bank of the River Thames has been a palace, a prison, a mint, a **menagerie**, and many other things. For nearly 1,000 years, at least one of its buildings has stood at that site, a watchful sentry, from the rule of William I the Conqueror right up to that of Elizabeth II.

Unsurprisingly, the tower has collected many stories over the years, from undeniably true history to more fanciful tales and ghost stories. With all the prisoners kept there and all the blood to stain those old stones, it's easy to imagine spirits lingering in the Tower of London. What do you think? Could the tower be haunted?

The Tower of London stands on the north bank of the River Thames. It's a World Heritage site.

THE TOWER RISES

William the Conqueror was a Norman (French) noble who rose to power and then invaded England. In 1066, he became king of England as William I. As someone who'd taken a throne by force himself, he knew he had to keep a strong hold on the country, especially the big city of London. So, William imported a practice from his homeland: he began to build a fortress, not only to protect the city but also to **intimidate** the people.

In 1078, workers began to build the central part of the tower, the White Tower. It was completed about 20 years later, but William I had already died. By 1154, his descendants no longer ruled England. It was, however, only the beginning for the Tower of London.

SPOOKY STUFF

THERE ARE TWO DIFFERENT STORIES ABOUT HOW THE WHITE TOWER GOT ITS NAME. SOME SAY IT WAS BECAUSE OF THE WHITE LIMESTONE USED TO BUILD IT, BUT SOME SAY KING HENRY III LATER HAD IT PAINTED WHITE.

The White Tower is 90 feet (27.4 m) high. It's roughly square, and each corner has its own tower.

-The First Prisoner-

The White Tower wasn't originally meant to be a prison, but it didn't take long before it was used as one. In 1100, King Henry I, a son of William I, had Ranulf Flambard, the bishop of Durham and an advisor of William II, arrested and imprisoned in the tower. However, Flambard escaped and fled the country—thus becoming the first person to escape the Tower of London as well.

GHOSTS WITH OPINIONS

So many kings and queens have added to the Tower of London over the years that it includes many different kinds of **architecture**. Other towers and walls rose around the central White Tower, particularly the additions of Kings Henry III and Edward I. One of the Tower of London's oldest ghost stories (if not its oldest) arose during Henry III's time, during the mid-1200s.

The story says that men were working on a wall when an angry ghost appeared and hit the wall with a cross. The wall collapsed! People believed this ghost was that of Thomas á Becket, archbishop of Canterbury, who'd been killed by followers of Henry III's grandfather. After that, the younger king had a chapel built in Becket's honor. The ghost was never seen again.

THOMAS Á BECKET WAS MADE A SAINT ABOUT THREE YEARS AFTER HIS DEATH IN 1170. THIS IS THE TRINITY CHAPEL, WHICH WAS BUILT TO BE HIS SHRINE.

BLOODY ROSES

One of the tower's most famous ghost stories was born… or, perhaps, died…in 1471. This was in the midst of the time of the Wars of the Roses, a series of civil wars between two families, the Yorks and the Lancasters, over the throne. Both families descended from King Edward III, and both thought they should rule.

King Henry VI—who'd held the throne, lost it, regained it, and lost it again during the wars—was imprisoned in the tower in 1471. On May 21, he was praying in a chapel in the Wakefield Tower when someone—perhaps the Duke of Gloucester—stabbed him to death. Now, stories say that every May 21, the **deposed** king's ghost walks around the chapel before fading again.

Despite the name, there's more than one tower in the Tower of London—in fact, there are many. Wakefield Tower was once the home of the kings of England.

-Start of the War-

Henry VI of the house of Lancaster took the English throne in 1422 when his father, Henry V, died. His rule wasn't a good one, and his relatives argued over power, causing a lot of chaos. Richard of York tried to take power himself, starting years of battle. Henry VI and his family eventually fled the country, but he returned in 1464 and the Yorks captured him, starting his first spell in the tower.

THE PRINCES IN THE TOWER

Another of the towers in the Tower of London was once known as the Garden Tower. However, many years later, that name changed. The story starts even further back, in 1483. That year, King Edward IV died suddenly, leaving behind two young sons: Edward, age 12, and Richard, age 10. Edward was to be King Edward V, and their uncle, Richard of Gloucester, sent them to the tower. He said it was until Edward could be crowned. But that never happened.

The elder Richard **usurped** the throne and was crowned King Richard III in July 1483. He got the British government to say neither of the young princes had the right to be king. And at some point later that year, the boys vanished.

THE PRINCES IN THE TOWER HAVE BEEN THE SUBJECTS OF MANY STORIES AND ARTWORK OVER THE YEARS. THEIR STORY HAS BEEN CALLED THE **ULTIMATE** COLD CASE.

-Richard III-

After he was crowned king, Richard III only ruled for two years before he was killed, defeated in battle by the future King Henry VII. For many years afterward, history and legend named Richard III as a bad and often wicked king. Even famous playwright William Shakespeare showed him as a villain in his play *Richard III*. However, today, historians think the truth probably wasn't quite that bad.

SKELETONS AND SPECTERS

No one knows exactly what happened to Edward V and his brother. Many people believe that Richard III had the boys murdered, although no one knows for sure. In 1674, workers found two small skeletons buried about 10 feet under a staircase in the White Tower. People believed the skeletons were those of the princes, and they were reburied in Westminster **Abbey**.

Guards in the tower say they've seen the shapes of two boys walking on the staircase, hand in hand. They're often said to be wearing white nightgowns. Others say they've seen the boys in the Garden Tower, now called the Bloody Tower. Some visitors to the tower say they've even taken photos of shadowy shapes or lights said to be the princes.

SPOOKY STUFF

The young princes could also have been killed on the orders of the future Henry VII, who had equal reasons to keep them from claiming the throne. In fact, he might have had more reason to do so.

In 1933, scientists examined the bones found in the White Tower. They concluded that they were of children the right age to be the princes.

At the Midnight Hour

One of the Tower of London's most legendary ghost stories is that of Anne Boleyn, the second wife of King Henry VIII. The king married her in January 1533, and they had a daughter, Elizabeth, in September 1533. However, Henry VIII didn't want a daughter. He wanted a son to take his throne. When Anne had no more living children, Henry lost interest in her. He wanted to take another wife. However, Anne was still alive.

Henry made up charges accusing Anne of many things, including witchcraft. On May 2, 1536, she was locked up in the Tower of London. Her stay was brief. On May 19, 1536, Anne Boleyn was found guilty and beheaded on the Tower Green. Henry married his next wife 11 days later.

These wax figures show Anne Boleyn with Henry VIII in the background. Their daughter became Queen Elizabeth I in 1558 and ruled England for many years.

-Remembered in Song-

A famous and memorable song, written in the 1930s, tells listeners how Anne Boleyn now haunts the Tower of London. Maybe you've heard it! It tells funny stories about how she haunted King Henry VIII and the tower after her execution. The chorus goes: "With her head tucked underneath her arm, She walks the bloody Tower, With her head tucked underneath her arm, At the midnight hour."

A TRAVELING GHOST

Anne Boleyn's death was just the start of many stories, however. She was buried in the Tower of London, underneath the current location of the chapel of Saint Peter ad Vincula. People say they've seen her ghost in many places in the tower, including the White Tower, the Tower Green (where she died), and the chapel.

However, if Anne haunts the Tower of London, she's not content to remain there. Those who believe in ghosts have claimed to see her spirit in locations throughout Great Britain. These places include Windsor Castle; Hever Castle in Kent, where she grew up; Blickling Hall in Norfolk; Salle Church in Norfolk; Marwell Hall in Hampshire, where Henry VIII may have been when Anne was killed; and Rochford Hall in Essex.

SPOOKY STUFF

Stories say that the ghost of Anne Boleyn goes to Blickling Hall every year on May 19, her execution day. She's said to arrive in a carriage with ghostly horses and a headless horseman.

Anne Boleyn's ghost is especially said to appear at Hever Castle, shown, on Christmas Eve or Christmas.

"I AM NO TRAITOR, NO, NOT I!"

Margaret Plantagenet was born in 1473, the niece of King Edward IV and a first cousin to the princes in the tower. As fate would have it, she lost her life there too, although it was much later. After Henry VII took the throne, the new king married Margaret off to make sure she wouldn't be a threat to his claim.

Over the years, Margaret became countess of Salisbury and wealthy in her own right. One of her sons, Reginald, became powerful in the Roman Catholic Church. When Henry VIII created the Church of England, in part so that he could get rid of his first wife and marry Anne Boleyn, Reginald spoke out against him. Henry was angry. He couldn't reach Reginald—but he *could* reach his mother.

MARGARET, WHO MARRIED SIR RICHARD POLE, WAS THEREAFTER KNOWN AS MARGARET POLE. ONE OF HER SONS, REGINALD, WAS THE ARCHBISHOP OF CANTERBURY.

Margaret Pole was imprisoned in the Tower of London in 1539. She was in her mid-60s, fairly old in that time. There she stayed for two years, until May 27, 1541, when Henry VIII ordered her execution without a trial or any charges. Some stories say that she refused to put her head on the block or that she tried to run away after the executioner missed her once. These may or may not be true, but Margaret did die there, beheaded on the Tower Green.

Today, visitors and guards at the tower sometimes say that Margaret's ghost appears on the anniversary of her death. It's said that she reenacts her last moments—sometimes trying to escape, still chased by the executioner.

SPOOKY STUFF

Tales say that Margaret Pole had a very inexperienced executioner—and that he had to hack at her neck and shoulders many times before he beheaded her.

-Margaret's Poem-

Some stories say that people found a poem carved into the wall of Margaret's cell in the Tower of London. Some believe she wrote it. It read:

For traitors on the block should die;
I am no traitor, no, not I!
My faithfulness stands fast and so,
towards the block I shall not go!
Nor make one step, as you shall see;
Christ in Thy Mercy, save Thou me!

Margaret Pole was made a **martyr** of the Catholic Church in 1886. This photo shows the Tower Green, where she died.

LADY JANE

With his third wife, Henry VIII finally had a son. When the king died in 1547, Edward VI, age 10, took the throne. However, he didn't have it for long. By 1553, the young king was very sick. He picked Jane Grey, the daughter-in-law of his adviser, as his heir instead of his half-sisters Mary (daughter of Henry VIII and Catherine of Aragon, his first wife) or Elizabeth. Jane was the great-granddaughter of King Henry VII.

Jane became queen on July 10, 1553. She reigned for nine days before Mary took power and threw Jane and her husband into prison in the tower. They were beheaded on February 12, 1554. Jane is often known as the Nine Days Queen. She was only 16 when she died.

-Lady in White-

Jane's tragic tale led to many stories of her ghost in the Tower of London. She's said to appear on the anniversary of her execution. Some people see her as a headless white shape. Other times, people have seen her floating from the mists of the River Thames. Visitors have also claimed to see the ghost of her husband, Lord Guildford Dudley, at the tower. The last reported sighting of Lady Jane was February 12, 1957.

Mary might have spared Jane and her husband after she took the throne, but then Jane's father took part in a rebellion against Mary. Jane's fate was sealed.

Lady Jane Grey

Spooky Stuff

Mary Tudor held the throne from 1553 to 1558. She was also known as Bloody Mary because of her **persecution** of people over religion. Many **Protestants** died under her reign.

"STRIKE, MAN, STRIKE!"

After Mary Tudor died, her half-sister, Elizabeth I reigned from 1558 to 1603. However, after Elizabeth I died without children, James I (who was also a descendant of King Henry VII) became king. Adventurer and writer Sir Walter Raleigh had been a favorite of Elizabeth's, but James I decided Sir Walter was plotting to overthrow him. The king imprisoned the other man in the Tower of London, where he spent the next 13 years.

In 1616, Sir Walter Raleigh was allowed to leave the tower to lead an expedition. However, his men attacked a colony against James I's orders. When Raleigh returned, the king had him beheaded. Reportedly, Raleigh told his executioner, "This is sharp medicine; but it is a sure cure for all diseases. What dost thou fear? Strike, man, strike."

Sir Walter Raleigh didn't die at the Tower of London but, perhaps because he spent so much time there, he's said to haunt it. People have reported seeing his ghost in many different tower locations.

CREATURES OF THE TOWER

For hundreds of years, from about the 1200s to the 1830s, the Tower of London housed the Royal Menagerie. Henry III started the collection of animals, many of which were gifts to British royalty. Later, Edward I had the so-called Lion Tower built to house the menagerie. James I later improved it. Over the years, the tower housed lions, tigers, a polar bear, an elephant, eagles, a jackal, monkeys, zebras, alligators, and kangaroos.

Most of the animals in the tower didn't live long, so it's probably not surprising to think they might have left angry ghosts there. In 1815, a guard said he saw a bear come out of a door in the tower. He attacked it, but his weapon went right through it!

Today, there are wire sculptures **depicting** the animals of the Royal Menagerie at the Tower of London.

-Ravens of the Tower-

Workers tore down the Lion Tower in the 1800s, and the surviving animals went to new homes. Still, one particular kind of animal still lives in the Tower of London today. An old legend says that if the resident ravens leave the tower, the tower and the kingdom itself will fall. There are seven ravens living there right now, and there's a special Ravenmaster who takes care of them.

SO MANY STORIES

These are only some of the ghost stories of the Tower of London. The tower's seen a lot of history, and that leads to many tales, both real and fanciful. For example, Guy Fawkes was a real man who took part in the Gunpowder Plot to blow up the British **Parliament** and King James I in 1605. It's true that he was held and tortured in the tower. But is it really true that his cries of anger and pain can still be heard there today?

Whether the ghost stories are true or not, they're fun to read and listen to. People can still visit the Tower of London today, climb its stairways, and walk those old stones. Whether there are ghosts there or not, their stories live on.

GLOSSARY

abbey: A church connected to buildings where religious personnel once lived.

architecture: A method or style of building.

depict: To show as.

depose: To remove a person from a position of power.

intimidate: To create a feeling of fear or awe in a person or animal.

martyr: Someone who dies for a cause.

menagerie: A collection of animals.

Parliament: The British lawmaking body.

persecution: Cruel treatment, especially because of a person's race or religious or political beliefs.

Protestant: A member of one of the Christian churches that separated from the Catholic Church in the 16th century.

ultimate: The greatest or most extreme of something.

usurp: To take and keep something away in a forceful way, if you don't have the right to do so.

INDEX

WEBSITES

Due to the changing nature of Internet links, PowerKids Press has developed an online list of websites related to the subject of this book. This site is updated regularly. Please use this link to access the list: www.powerkidslinks.com/haunted/london